CELEBRATION STORIES

The Treasure of
Santa Cruz

SAVIOUR PIROTTA

Illustrated by Kathryn Prewett

HODDER
Wayland

an imprint of Hodder Children's Books

Celebrating Easter

Easter is the holiest and most important date in the Christian year. It is always celebrated in spring. During the Easter festivities, Christians celebrate the day when Jesus was raised from the dead after dying on the cross.

Before Easter comes a period of forty days known as Lent. This is a time when people from the Christian faith think about how they can lead better lives. Most of them give up some kind of luxury, such as sweets or meat. This helps them to think more carefully about the suffering that Jesus was about to undergo and that there are more important things in life than luxuries.

The last week of Lent is known as Holy Week. It starts with Palm Sunday, when Christians celebrate the day Jesus went to Jerusalem for the Jewish festival of Passover and was hailed as a king by the crowds.

In many countries, people mark the day with processions and ceremonies in which they carry palm leaves or olive branches.

The Friday following Palm Sunday is known as Good Friday. It is the day when Jesus died on the cross. Many Christians spend the day fasting and praying. In some countries, there are colourful pageants showing the story of the passion of Jesus. There are also sombre ceremonies in churches and at places of pilgrimage.

Easter traditionally begins in the dark hours before dawn on the following Sunday morning. This is the time when Christians remember how Jesus' friends found his tomb empty. After the long days of Lent and the sadness of Good Friday, Christians can celebrate joyfully. There are special ceremonies, church bells are rung and festive foods are eaten.

Hopes and Dreams

It was the last day of school before the Easter
holidays. We were meant to be doing maths but
we'd already put our books away and tidied the
classroom. Miss Flores, our teacher, told us to
sit at our desks.

"Are you all looking forward to the fiestas?"
she asked.

"Yes," the whole class said together. Our seaside town of Santa Cruz is very proud of its fiestas, especially the festivals of *Semana Santa*, the Holy Week. They start with a solemn procession on Palm Sunday and finish with the noisy celebrations of Easter Day.

Miss Flores looked at one of the girls sitting at the front. "Are you taking part in the festivals?" she asked her.

"I'm carrying an olive branch in the Palm Sunday procession," answered the girl, whose name was Carmen.

Some of the other children held up their hands. "I'm singing in the choir, Miss," said one, and, "My father is dressing up as a Roman soldier," said another.

Miss Flores smiled at me. "And you, Salvador," she said, "are you doing anything in one of the festivals?"

"I'm hoping to take part in the Good Friday pageant," I answered.

The Good Friday pageant was the biggest
festival of the *Semana Santa*. People dressed
as characters from the Bible paraded along the
streets of Santa Cruz. Men carried big statues
showing the story of Jesus' passion. The town
children held lanterns and candles.

But I wasn't hoping to carry a lantern or a candle. I wanted the best job in the whole of the *Semana Santa.*

"He wants to carry the cross of Santa Cruz, Miss," said Carmen.

Every year one ten-year-old boy in the town was chosen to carry a huge golden cross at the head of the Good Friday procession. It was a precious relic, studded with diamonds and rubies. No one in Santa Cruz knew how it had come to be in our parish church, although there was a local legend that said angels had brought it to the city in the Middle Ages.

We kids called it the treasure of Santa Cruz and we all wanted to carry it on Good Friday.

"Juan wants to carry the cross, too," continued Carmen, who seemed very well informed about everybody's hopes and dreams.

Juan was my best friend and we did everything together.

"Well, only one boy will get the honour of carrying the cross," said Miss Flores.

"It's always the boys who get to take part in the Good Friday pageant," complained Carmen. "It's about time the girls got a look-in, too. It's not fair!"

The other girls murmured in agreement.

Just then we heard the jangle of the home-time bell. As we filed out of the classroom, Juan and I smiled at each other. "It doesn't matter which one of us gets to carry the cross," said Juan. "We're friends, right?"

"Right," I said.

The Golden Cross

The man who chose which boy was going to carry the cross of Santa Cruz was Don Francisco, an old priest with white hair and thick glasses. He was in charge of all the town's fiestas.

"Ten other boys have applied to carry the cross," said Juan as we made our way to the parish church.

"But none of them have worked as hard for Don Francisco as we have," I said.

"True," agreed Juan. The old priest liked to reward the hardest-working boy in the parish by letting him carry the precious cross.

When we got to the church, we made our way to the sacristy at the back. The room was full of people, all waiting to hear what their role in the various pageants was going to be. Some of the boys looked at us nervously as we took a seat. They knew that both Juan and I were high on Don Francisco's list.

The door to the priest's office opened and a group of men walked out.

"Hey, Papa," said Juan.

My friend's father beamed at us. "I've been chosen to carry the statue of the Risen Christ on Easter Sunday," he said.

Juan and I gasped. That was the biggest honour of all. Everybody in the town wanted to do it but only eight men were chosen every year. They carried the statue on their shoulders, four at the front and four at the back. Juan and I had already promised each other that one day we, too, would carry the Risen Christ.

Don Francisco cleared his throat to get everybody's attention. A hush fell on the room. The old priest blinked at a piece of paper in his hand.

"Pablo, Ricardo, Julio, Eusebio, Paco and Juan will each carry a lantern. The rest of you will carry candles, two in front of every statue."

He turned to me, taking off his glasses. "Salvador Jimenez will carry the golden cross. Congratulations, Salvador."

I was over the moon. Me, Salvador Jimenez, carrying the treasure of Santa Cruz like my father before me and my grandfather before him.

I raced home to tell my mother. "You *must* take pictures of me," I said, "and make a video."

"Calm down, Salvador," said my mother, laughing. "What is Juan going to do in the festival?"

"He's carrying a lantern," I said. I turned to my friend, who had followed me home.

"Congratulations," he said for the fifth time, beaming. I could tell that he wasn't jealous of my good luck. He truly was pleased for me. I could see it in his face.

Salvador's Pride

The next day Juan and I went to see Señora de Santos. It was her job to make sure that the ancient Holy Week costumes properly fitted the people in the pageants. As Juan and I skipped along the streets, friends and relatives appeared in doorways to congratulate me.

"Look after that cross," they said.

"Don't drop it, will you!"

My chest swelled with pride. Everyone in the town seemed to know that I had been chosen to carry the cross.

At Señora de Santos' house I tried on my costume, a red velvet robe with a thick, blue sash. Señora de Santos tucked up the hem with pins, then folded the sleeves over so they did not flap against my hands.

"I'll take it up this afternoon," she said, "and I'll bring it round to your house later in the week."

Juan tried on his costume, too. It wasn't as grand as mine, of course, just a black robe trimmed with white lace. When we had finished, we set off home.

23

As we turned the corner on to our street, we heard sobbing. A crowd had gathered outside Juan's house. We saw Juan's mum crying, her hands held to her face. My mum was consoling her. A policeman was writing something in a notebook.

When we approached the crowd, we saw Carmen. "It's Juan's father," she whispered, her eyes full of concern. "He's missing."

The Storm

Juan's father was a fisherman. He caught lobsters and swordfish to sell to the restaurants in Santa Cruz. Juan often went out fishing with him, to help lace the water with bait. But not in rough weather. There had been a storm the night before. I'd heard the wind howling outside my window and the waves breaking on the shore.

Beside me, Juan had gone deathly pale. His hands were trembling.

"We found the boat washed up on shore," said the policeman to no one in particular. "A few kilometres up the coast."

A neighbour helped Juan's mother into the house and Juan followed her.

I said goodbye and crossed the street to our house, hoping against hope that the policeman was wrong.

"He will be all right, Papa, won't he?" I said to my dad.

"I just don't know, son," he said sadly. "They've searched all over the coast, and out to sea, too, with helicopters."

Don Francisco's Request

Two days later, Señora de Santos came round with my costume. I tried it on in front of the mirror. For a moment I forgot Juan's tragedy. In my mind's eye, I could see people watching me as I carried the golden cross. There was Don Francisco, and Miss Flores nodding at me. And my mum taking pictures. Yes, I would carry the treasure of Santa Cruz with pride.

A knock at the door made me jump.

"Salvador," my mum called out. "There's someone to see you."

I took off the robe and went into the front room. Don Francisco was sitting in our best chair, drinking a glass of lemonade.

"I want to speak to you, Salvador," he said.

I sat down in another chair.

"I'm concerned about Juan," said Don Francisco. "He's taking the loss of his father very badly. His mother tells me that he's been having nightmares. He hasn't slept since last Saturday. Why don't you let him carry the golden cross, Salvador? It might take his mind off things."

I stood up, panic building in my mind.
"I can't," I gasped. "I worked hard all year for
the honour and I'm not going to give it away."

"Salvador," my mother said gently.

"No way!" I shouted, and ran out the door.

I walked for hours. It wasn't fair. Just when
something had gone right for me, I had to give
it up. I tried to tell myself that Juan didn't really
want to carry the cross. He was happy for me
to carry it. After all, he had other things on
his mind.

But, deep in my heart, I knew that Don Francisco was right. Having the honour of carrying the treasure of Santa Cruz would give Juan something to look forward to.

Except it was so difficult to give up something you've wanted all your life.

I just couldn't do it. I was going to carry the cross of Santa Cruz on Good Friday.

A White Lie

I didn't see Juan for the next two days. The town was busy preparing for Good Friday. All the paintings in the parish church were covered in black cloth as a sign of mourning for Jesus' death. The church bells were muffled in thick drapes. They would not ring again until Easter, when Jesus was risen from the dead.

Meanwhile, I hung around listlessly. Things just weren't the same without Juan.

I decided to go and see him. I made my way down to the harbour and found him sitting alone in his father's boat, his fishing rod in his hands.

"Are you OK?" I asked.

He shrugged, his eyes fixed on the line.

"It's Good Friday tomorrow," I said. "Are you looking forward to the pageant?"

Juan nodded but still didn't speak.

"I miss you," I said suddenly.

Juan turned round to face me. He had tears running down his cheek. He must have been crying a long time because his eyes were all red and puffy. I couldn't bear it. I'd seen my best friend crying before, but not like this, not with so much pain.

"I've come to tell you something," I said. "You can carry the golden cross instead of me, if you want."

I saw a flicker of surprise on Juan's face. "I can't do that," he said. "You've wanted to carry that cross all your life."

I had to convince him somehow. "You know I broke my arm last year when I fell over during football at school. I don't think my arm can take the weight of the cross," I said, hoping that he'd believe me. "You'd be doing me a favour, Juan, honestly."

The Procession

It was Good Friday. The procession had started, with Juan carrying the cross at its head. The whole village had turned out to see us walking with a measured pace along the streets of Santa Cruz. There were people carrying the statues, with us boys holding lanterns on either side of them. Behind us were men dressed as Roman soldiers and women singing mournful songs.

As we turned into the main square, the evening light made the jewels on the cross sparkle. The crowd gasped in amazement. I couldn't help feeling a bit jealous as people admired my friend rather than me.

"Next year I'm going to carry the golden cross," I whispered to Carmen, who was watching the pageant with her family.

"You won't be allowed to," said Carmen brightly.

"Why not?" I laughed. "Have the girls decided to take over next year?"

"No," she replied. "Don Francisco always chooses a boy our age to carry the cross. It's the tradition. You'll be too old next year."

I was stunned. Why hadn't I thought of that before telling Juan he could carry the cross? Now I'd lost my chance for ever. I would be the first Jimenez in the family never to have carried the treasure of Santa Cruz.

As we crossed the square, the wind making the lights in our lanterns dance crazily, I felt tears of frustration running down my face.

"Fool," I said to myself.

The Real Treasure

It was Saturday, that quiet day between Good Friday and Easter Sunday when we think of Jesus lying dead in his tomb. Mum and I were making Easter cakes. I was careful not to eat sugar as I worked the dough. The cakes were meant for Sunday, when we celebrated Jesus rising from the dead. As I was washing my hands at the sink, we heard people shouting outside.

"It's Juan's father – he's safe!"

Mum and I rushed outside. People were knocking at Juan's door.

"They found him on an island out to sea," a woman told us. "He was unconscious but alive. They've taken him to the hospital."

Juan's mother opened the door and came out. She screamed when she heard the news and tears of joy ran down her face. Juan grinned at me. Soon the whole town seemed to be crammed on our street, laughing and cheering. It felt like Easter already.

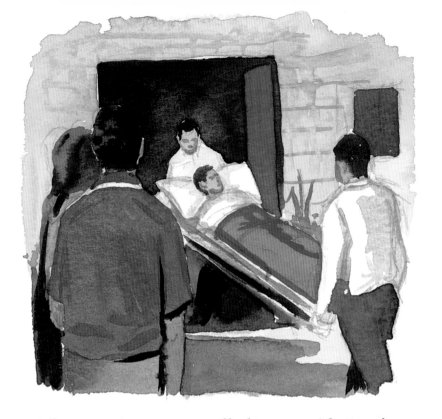

That evening, a van pulled up outside Juan's
house. It had a red cross on it, so I knew it was
from the hospital. The neighbours gathered
round as Juan's father was lifted out of it and
carried into the house on a stretcher.

The neighbours followed, chattering excitedly.
Don Francisco was with them, shaking his head
and laughing.

"Salvador," someone called out. "Where is
Salvador? Juan's father wants to speak to him."

I pushed my way to the front of the crowd. Juan's father was sitting up in his bed, his back against a white pillow. He looked pale and tired but he seemed to be on the mend.

"Juan told me what you did," he said.

I blushed, remembering how I had regretted it afterwards.

"You are a true friend," continued Juan's father. "I would like to give you a gift. You are tall for your age, and strong like your father. How about taking my place and carrying the statue of the Risen Christ, tomorrow? After all, I am in no state to carry anything."

I couldn't believe my ears. No kid had ever been allowed to carry the statue of the Risen Christ before. It was too precious for children to handle.

"You deserve it, Salvador," said Don Francisco behind me.

Everyone in the room started clapping. I went as red as one of my mum's beetroots. Me, Salvador Jimenez, carrying the statue of the Risen Christ with the other men of Santa Cruz, the first boy in the town ever to do so!

I hugged Juan. I was so glad that he was my best friend.

Don Francisco smiled and nodded at me. "I'm proud of you, Salvador," he whispered. "You gave up something very important to you to help a friend. It's what Easter is all about."

At that moment I realized that the real treasure of Santa Cruz was not the jewel-encrusted cross in the church. It was the love all us villagers felt for one another.

Glossary

Fiesta A celebration.

Good Friday The day that Jesus died on the cross.

Holy Week A week of Christian activity, starting with Palm Sunday and ending with Easter.

Pageant A parade, usually performed outside.

Palm Sunday The first day of Holy Week, when Christians celebrate the entry of Jesus into Jerusalem.

Passion The suffering and death of Jesus.

Relic An object that has been used by a holy person.

Sacristy The back part of a church where priests get ready for ceremonies.

Semana Santa The Spanish name for Holy Week.

CELEBRATION STORIES

Look out for these other titles in the Celebration Stories series:

A Present For Salima by Kerena Marchant
It's Ramadan, and Ibrahim is allowed to fast like the adults do – as long as he drinks water during the day. So when he travels to the mountains with his father, he stops at a small village for a drink. Ibrahim is shocked to discover how hard it is for Salima and the other villagers to get water. He realizes he has a lot to be thankful for. He really wants to help – but how?

The Dragon Doorway by Clare Bevan
Nothing's going right for Nathan's family – Dad's broken his big toe, the roof's leaking, and Mum's lost her pantomime job as Goldy the Magic Chicken... So when a competition leaflet comes through the door, promising a family ticket for a mystery tour, Nathan thinks it's worth a try. All he's got to do is solve a riddle. But no one seems to have a clue – until Nathan finds the Dragon Doorway...

Waiting For Elijah by Ann Jungman
Debbie has always asked the four questions at the Passover meal – it's her favourite part. So when she finds out that her younger cousin will be doing it this year, Debbie's upset. Worse still, she has to open the door to the Prophet Elijah instead – and he never comes. But then a new friend helps her to realize that opening the door to Elijah is more important than she thinks.

You can buy all these books from your local bookseller, or order them direct from the publisher. For more information about Celebration Stories, write to: *The Sales Department, Hodder Children's Books, a division of Hodder Headline Limited, 338 Euston Road, London NW1 3BH.*